When I Was Big

by Debbie Kaplan

When I Was Big
Copyright © 2010 ECKANKAR

Printed in USA
Illustrated by Keit Osadchuk
Edited by Patrick Carroll, Joan Klemp, and Anthony Moore

Library of Congress Cataloging-in-Publication Data
Kaplan, Debbie.
    When I was big / by Debbie Kaplan ; [illustrated by Keit Osadchuk].
        p. cm.
    ISBN 978-1-57043-318-4 (pbk. : alk. paper) 1. Reincarnation--Eckankar (Organization)--Juvenile literature. 2. Eckankar (Organization)--Doctrines--Juvenile literature. I. Osadchuk, Keit. II. Title.
    BP605.E3K37 2010
    299'.93--dc22
                                2009052801

∞ This paper meets the requirements of ANSI/NISO Z39.48-1992 (Permanence of Paper).

Hi, I am Davie.

Come along with me
to see some of my Past Lives,
as we look at
When I was BIG.

When I was BIG

I baked cakes and pies in a castle for a King and Queen.

When
I was
BIG

I worked on a ship
and sailed around
the world.

When I was BIG

I taught children in a school with a big bell on the top.

Now I am little again, just like you. We have all come back here to Earth to share another lifetime together, for you and I are Soul, a Spark of God's Love.

God has sent us here again to his schoolhouse called Earth. We have all come back to learn and grow.

We go to school many, many times to have new adventures and to learn more lessons of LOVE.

For Further Reading, Study, and Fun

Illustrated ECK Parables

by Harold Klemp

A Gift for the Master
It Matters to This Starfish
Nubby and Sunshine
One Small Thing for Love
The Song That Makes God Happy
Struggle of the Emperor Moth

Harold Klemp's parables have brought spiritual wisdom and inspiration to seekers everywhere. Now available in beautiful, full-color booklets illustrated by artist Amanda Gunz, these parables will be treasured by youth of all ages.

Also available are CDs, each of which contains a PowerPoint slide show of three illustrated parables for use in events for youth. *Illustrated ECK Parables CD 1* includes *It Matters to This Starfish, Nubby and Sunshine,* and *Struggle of the Emperor Moth. Illustrated ECK Parables CD 2* contains *A Gift for the Master, One Small Thing for Love,* and *The Song That Makes God Happy.*

Available from Eckankar: www.Eckankar.org; (952) 380-2222; ECKANKAR, Dept. BK90, PO Box 2000, Chanhassen, MN 55317-2000 USA.